The Bremen Town Musicians

In a distant land, a man had a donkey. He served the man for many years, carrying sacks to the mill. But due to old age the donkey was unable to work anymore. His master thought that it was useless to feed him. Fearing that his master would kill him, one day the donkey ran away. He went towards Bremen, where he thought he would become a town musician.

When the donkey had gone a little way, he found a hunting dog lying by the side of the road panting as if he was very tired.
'Why are you panting my friend?' asked the donkey.
'As I am old and weak, I can no longer go hunting. For this reason my master wanted to kill me, so I ran away. But now I'm worried how I will earn my bread, said the dog.'

'That is indeed very pitiful,' said the donkey thoughtfully. 'I am going to Bremen to become a town musician there. Come along with me. I'll play the flute and you can beat the drums.' The dog was happy to hear this. He accompanied the donkey and they went further.

It didn't take them long before they came to a cat who was sitting sadly by the roadside. 'What happened my dear friend?' asked the donkey kindly.

'Oh, I am getting old, and my teeth are no longer sharp. I cannot chase mice as I used to do earlier. So my mistress wanted to drown me, but I ran away. But where will I go now?'

'Come with us to Bremen. You can become a town musician there,' said the donkey. The cat agreed and went along. Then the three travellers came to a farmyard. The rooster of the house was sitting on the gate and crying with all his might. 'What's wrong my friend?' asked the donkey. 'Why are you crying so loudly?'

'Tomorrow is Sunday and guests are coming. The lady of the house has no mercy. She has told the cook that she wants to eat me tomorrow. So I am supposed to let them kill me this evening. That's why I'm crying as loudly as I can,' said the rooster, sadly.

'My dear Red Head, instead of staying here, come with us. We're going to Bremen. You have a good voice and when we make music together, it will be very pleasing,' said the donkey. The rooster was happy with the proposal. And so, all the four friends went off together.

However, they could not reach the city of Bremen in one day. It was evening when they came reached a forest. They decided to spend the night there. The donkey and the dog lay down under a big tree, and the cat and the rooster took to the branches of the same tree. The rooster flew right to the top, so that he could see far off things.

Before falling asleep the rooster looked around carefully in all the four directions and he saw a little spark burning at a distance. 'That must be a house not too far from here,' he said to his friends.

The donkey said, 'Then we must go there, because sleeping like this is pretty difficult.' They all agreed to this and moved towards the place where the light was coming from. Soon they came to an old cottage.

As the donkey was the tallest of them all, he looked through the window. All his friends eagerly waited for him.

'Friend, what do you see? asked the rooster excitedly.

'What do I see? I see a table set with delicious food and four robbers enjoying themselves,' answered the donkey.

'I am sure there will be something for us. Why don't we drive those robbers away and enjoy the food?' suggested the rooster.

Then the four friends discussed how they could drive the robbers away. At last they thought of a plan.

According to their plan, the donkey stood on the window with his front feet, the dog jumped onto the donkey's back and the cat climbed onto the dog. Finally, the rooster flew up and sat on the cat. After taking their positions, they began to call out together, loudly.
The donkey BRAYED, the dog BARKED, the cat MEOWED and the rooster CROWED.

Then they crashed through the window into the room shattering the panes in the cottage! The robbers fled into the woods in great fear thinking there was a ghost. The four friends merrily feasted on the leftovers.

When the four friends had eaten their fill, they put out the light and went to sleep. The donkey lay down in the farmyard, the dog behind the door, the cat on the hearth and the rooster sat on the beam of the roof. Soon they fell asleep.

Later that night, the robbers saw that the light was no longer glowing in the house and there was complete silence. They sent one of the robbers to the house.

The poor man went into the kitchen first to strike a light. He mistook the cat's glowing eyes for burning coals. He held a match to them. The cat was angry and scratched his face badly.

Frightened, the man ran towards the back door, where the dog bit him in the leg. When he ran across the yard, the donkey kicked him hard and the rooster cried, 'Cock-a-doodle-doo!'

The robber ran back to the house and said, 'Oh, there is a horrible WITCH in the house! She scratched my face with her long nails and stabbed me in the leg. A black monster lying in the yard struck me with its club. And the judge sitting up on the roof called out, 'Bring the rogue here! I ran away as fast as I could.'

From that time, the robbers did not dare to go back to the house and the four friends lived there happily.